TEXTIN' UP MY HEART

TEAGAN HUNTER

My readers,
Thank you for loving Zach and Delia so much.
This one is for you.

CHAPTER 1

I ROLL over to face the adorable, albeit idiotic, guy lying next to me.

Back pressed against the headboard, leg bent, phone in hand, he shoots me the grin I've loved since the moment I met him. "Good morning."

I quirk a brow. "Did you just text me to ask if I'm awake when I am *right* next to you?"

"Yeah, but it's not weird." He lifts a shoulder and shakes his phone at me. "Texting is our thing."

"Our thing or not, it's weird."

His grin widens, his panty-dropping dimples poking through. "You love it, and me."

"You're not wrong." I push myself up, brushing back my unruly, long brown hair. "Why are you up so early?"

"I'm bored. There's nothing to do."

"This might sound crazy, but you could try, I dunno, *sleeping*. Especially since it's only"—I glance at the clock Zach keeps on the bedside table for "nostalgia"—"7:30...on a Saturday."

"It's 7:30? Crap! I slept in!" Tossing his phone down onto the bed, he launches up onto his feet, clapping his hands together excitedly. "Let's do this!"

My eyes fall to slits at his unexpected enthusiasm. If there's one thing Zach loves, it's sleep. He's never up before nine on the weekends.

"What's wrong with you? What's going on? Are you sick?" I gasp. "Do you have cancer? Because we aren't married and I'm not on your life insurance."

"I'm not sick, and I'll add you to my life insurance if you want."

"You will?"

"Yes." His voice is steady and sure, unwavering as he drops his hands to his hips and stands there in nothing but his Deadpool boxer briefs, the morning sunlight glowing around him like a halo. My man might be the biggest nerd I've ever met—building apps in his basement, devouring comic books whenever he's not busy, and buying the most expensive tickets to whatever nerdy convention is in town—but damn does he know how to take care of his body. His dark brows furrow as he continues, "Why the hell wouldn't I? You're my girl, Delia."

"Your girl?"

"Yeah, you know...my love. My boo. My old lady. My bae."

"Don't ever call me your bae."

"Fine, *bae*. I won't, *bae*."

I glare at him. "I will murder you. I'm not scared of prison. Prison should be scared of *me*."

"That's a fair assessment." He waves a hand. "Anyway, yes, I'll put you on my life insurance, mostly because if you *do* kill me, I'll have deserved it, and I want to make sure I leave you with a little something-something to make up for being a total douche."

My lips curve up. "That's actually kind of sweet. Now tell me what's wrong with you."

"Nothing. I'm just really jazzed today."

"Jazzed? *Jazzed?* Nobody says jazzed, Zachary."

He glares at me when I use his fake full name. "Jazzed," he whispers with faux menace.

"Seriously, what's going on? You're never up this early on weekends. You said they were 'your turn to damn the man and save the empire'...whatever that means."

"That record store is a national treasure!" He shakes his fist. "National treasure, Delia!"

I sigh and roll my eyes at his antics because, much like he's been doing for a few weeks now, he's avoiding the question when I ask him if something is wrong.

"Zach..."

"Delia..." he mocks, brow raised, smirk lining his lips.

"What's going on?"

The brow drops, his lips falling into a frown when he realizes I'm not playing around.

"Nothing's going on," he says quickly...*too* quickly. I study him and his eyes dart off to the corner of the room, uncomfortable under my scrutiny. "J-Just ready for the day is all." He claps his hands together in excitement. "What do we have planned?"

"Well, I was hoping we could chill in bed, maybe snuggle on the couch like bums. Or bang. Feels like it's been weeks since I've seen you."

He sighs. "You see me every night, Delia."

Technically speaking, he's right. I *do* see him every night, but lately it doesn't always *feel* like he's there. He's been so into whatever's happening on his screen lately that I'm actually starting to feel jealous of a device.

"True, but your phone is always glued to your hand. If I didn't know how much you value your balls, I'd say you were cheating on me."

"One, I *do* love my balls, but that's not why I'm not cheating on you. I'm not cheating on you because I love you. Two, I'm sorry. I've just been...working some kinks out. It'll be better soon, I promise. Stop being jealous."

"I'm not jealous."

He raises his eyebrows.

"Fine, fine. You're right. I'm just being silly, I guess."

"You are." He leans forward and kisses my head again before pushing off the bed completely. "I'm gonna go make some breakfast, then we gotta get moving on the day."

"It's a Saturday. Remind me why we need to get out of bed at all?"

"Did you forget? We're having a barbeque today."

"We are?"

"Yep."

"Since when?"

"Since I decided. We're doing burgers and potato salad and asparagus...all the fun, usual shit."

I crinkle my nose at him. "Do you even know what people eat at barbeques? Because asparagus isn't a typical cookout menu item."

"It is now."

"I knew it—you *are* sick!"

Ignoring me, he crosses the room to the dresser, and I cry a little on the inside when he pulls out a shirt, covering up his chiseled chest. He pulls our bedroom door open. "Eggs, bacon, toast, and carrots okay with you?"

"Carrots?! Sick, sick, sick!"

He laughs.

"Just tell me if it's cancer!" I yell after him. "And what color ribbon I need to wear!"

Zach: Are you dressed yet?

Me: No. I went back to bed.

Zach: DELIA DEVLIN

Zach: YOU GET YOUR CUTE ASS OUT HERE RIGHT NOW

Zach: Robbie and Monty will be here any minute

Me: OMG you were serious about the barbeque?!

Zach: YES!

Me: DAMMIT ZACHARY!

I THOUGHT he was just joking this morning, though the moment I finished the last bite of my toast, he stole my plate and disappeared to go prepare for our guests. Annoyed, I sank into the cozy king bed once the door clicked shut, and then the food coma set in. I surrendered to it, letting my eyes close for a quick nap to shut out all the thoughts running through my head.

According to my phone, that was two hours ago.

I spring up from the bed that's beckoning to me, giving it a longing look as I try to rack my brain on my why Zach is so hellbent on having a damn barbeque today.

I don't want to people. I just want to be lazy.

More specifically, I want to be lazy with him.

"I'm up!" I shout.

"Good, you bum!" he retorts.

Racing around the room, I stuff a pair of jeans and a plain top into my hands before rushing off toward the bathroom. I turn the handle on the shower and make quick work of wrangling my long tresses into a messy bun—no time to wash *and* dry this mess—before stripping and hopping under the hot stream of water.

I don't dawdle, because I know if I do, Zach will be in here wondering what the hell I'm doing, asking if I'm "flicking the bean to thoughts of him."

I'm washed and dried in ten minutes and pulling on my clothes just as the doorbell rings.

"You hear that, Delia?" Zach shouts from the

doorway of our bedroom as I struggle to get my bra snapped, my still-wet-and-sticky skin making it difficult to get the hooks lined up. "Our guests are here! Put your titties away!"

"I will do as I please with my titties!"

His laughter trickles down the hall as the hooks finally snap into place, and I quickly pull my shirt over my head as I hear him let his best friend and his drop-dead gorgeous fiancée inside.

A pang of envy fills my chest when I think of the lovebirds, not because I want Robbie or anything—*gross, he's like my brother*—but because of that rock sitting atop Monty's finger.

I never thought I was the type of girl to give a shit about marriage. I didn't fantasize about my wedding as a little girl. I've always firmly been in the "If it happens, it happens" camp. Even after I met Zach and decided to move in with him, I still felt that way.

Until last month.

The gang got together for dinner, Robbie and Monty using the opportunity to announce their upcoming nuptials. For the first time ever, I was covetous of what my friends had and I didn't—namely, a promise for a future.

I pushed it aside as nothing more than a fleeting moment of green...until earlier this week as I sat on the toilet, peeing on a stick because my period is over two weeks late.

Those three minutes were agonizing, and I breathed a sigh of relief when the test came back negative.

Then, I cried.

I wasn't sad because I wasn't pregnant, but because I realized if I were pregnant, Zach and I had no solid plan for our future. We haven't talked about babies or marriage or anything big. We've just been...well, together, and suddenly all these questions began rolling through my head.

What happens if do get pregnant? Will Zach be mad? Will we have to get married? It's been five years—how are we not married yet? Why hasn't Zach proposed?

Which of course spiraled into something even worse.

What if he doesn't love me like he once did? What if we're at a standstill? What if we don't last? Will we have to raise our baby in separate households? Who gets the goats?

Once the seeds of doubt were planted, they grew, and I started questioning everything about our relationship.

Is this barbeque just an excuse to not be around me? Why is he kissing my forehead so much? Did he change his cologne? Is that a sign he wants change? Are we not stable anymore? Did he burn my toast because he doesn't think about me like I think about him?

I mean, I know the answer to the last one—Zach sucks at breakfast—but the burnt toast is the least of my worries.

What really concerns me is the fact that in the last several years, despite all the steps our friends are taking in their relationships, it feels like Zach and are still just...well, us.

That isn't a bad thing, because he's great.

It's just, for the first time ever, I want *more*.

I *want* to get married. I *want* to purchase a home that's completely ours. I *want* to draw up our wills and get really damn serious about our future. I want to do all the husband-and-wife things.

As silly as it sounds, I want the piece of paper saying he's mine forever.

I just have no idea how to tell him that.

Groaning at the juvenile thought, I give my head a shake and finish securing my hair into another messy bun—this one slightly cleaner than the last—then swipe on a few layers of mascara, doing everything I can to send those thoughts away.

I walk out of the bedroom just as Robbie clambers up the stairs.

"I swear, if I walk in here and your titties are hanging out..."

"What is everyone's obsession with my breasts today?"

Robbie peers up at me, a devilish grin on his full lips. "Need any help with those?"

"Need any help with that grave you're digging for yourself?"

He snorts. "Please. Like you could take me."

"Whatcha doing up here, big guy?"

"Zach wanted me to ask if you know where his apron is." His lips twitch at the question, and I know it's because he thinks his best friend's kitchen getup is as ridiculous as I do. "And where did you want the slip and slide?"

"Oh, is Xavie here?"

Xavier, Robbie's son, has become such a constant in our life, it almost feels like Zach and I share custody of him sometimes.

That's not me complaining. I love that little shit like he's my own, which is good, because although I'd like to become Zach's wife, that's about as traditional as I get with life.

I do *not* want kids. Zach's a big enough handful on his own.

"Hell no. I wouldn't set up a slide just for that little

punk. Between Zach, you, and Monty, he's spoiled enough as it is."

"Says the father who spoils him the most."

Robbie ignores my jab because he knows I'm right. "He's at his mom's for the weekend. This is for us grownups."

"A slip and slide? Seriously? Whose genius idea was that?"

Robbie's mouth tilts up in one corner, and I hold up a hand, shaking my head.

"Never mind. I already know."

"He's your boyfriend," he reminds me.

"Yeah, and who do I have to blame for that?"

He laughs. "Fair enough."

Nearly five years ago, Robbie wrote down the wrong number for a client. Zach, being the good businessman he is, followed through on the callback...only it was me who answered.

The rest, as they say, is history.

Well, minus a naked photo scandal and a baby goat...or three.

It still amazes me some days when I stop to think about it. All because of one messed-up digit, I met the one person in the world who gets me on a level that astounds me daily.

He doesn't care if I eat half a pizza in one sitting or

devour a pan of brownies like I'll never eat again. He doesn't laugh—well, not too hard—at my hideous Ryan Gosling pajamas or care that I'd rather knit or play bingo than go out to the clubs even though I'm still in my twenties.

Zach Hastings gets me, and I'm lucky enough to get him in return.

"Are you really just gonna stand in front of me with a dopey-as-shit smile on your face having sex daydreams about my best friend? You're a sick creature, Delia."

I snap out of my haze and twist my lips up. "Not everything is about sex, Robbie!"

"Can you please say it louder for him? I've been trying to get that through his thick skull since the day I met him."

Robbie spins on the stairs toward his fiancée, his hand coming up to capture her jaw. He runs a thumb across her plump bottom lip. "I don't hear you complaining about all the sex, Monts."

"No!" I shout, pushing past them. "Nope! Not standing there while you two do...whatever that is."

"Foreplay," Robbie says nonchalantly.

I groan because it's like hearing a sibling talk about their sex life. "Gross. Just don't bang on our bed, please." *Or do. It could use the action.*

On top of Zach being attached to his phone lately, we haven't had sex in weeks.

And I miss sex.

I miss my boyfriend.

Fucking hell, Delia. Quit being dramatic.

I hit the bottom of the stairs, plastering my back against the wall.

Your boyfriend loves you. Your boyfriend wants you. You're just being dumb because you still haven't had your period. It's hormones. You're freaking out for nothing. Chill.

Monty's playful giggles penetrate my thoughts, and I'm brought back to earth.

I give myself a shake and paste on a smile.

I will not freak out today because there's a chance my boyfriend doesn't want to marry me. I will not freak out.

Will. Not.

Maybe if I say it enough times, it'll come true.

CHAPTER 2

MAKING my way through the living room, I grab the laundry basket Zach left sitting on the couch as I pass by and move into the kitchen.

Zach's standing at the counter, head dropped, attention fully on his phone. He's so absorbed in whatever he's doing he doesn't even acknowledge me entering.

I barely hold back the sigh I want to release. I swear every time I've walked into the room for the last month, he's been on that damn thing. I get it, work is important, but it's a Saturday for crying out loud. He can afford to put the phone down for a minute.

"Here. Heard you were looking for this." I pull out the apron Zach's looking for and toss it onto the counter as I head for the laundry room, where I drop the basket onto the dryer before closing the door behind me and wandering back into the kitchen.

"Sweet! Thank you." He abandons his phone, wrapping the apron around his waist.

I lean against the counter, watching him, my tongue darting out to wet my lips as he ties the material behind his back.

"Ha! I knew you secretly loved this apron!"

"You're wearing the naked chest of Ryan Reynolds right now." I lift a shoulder. "How can I not love it?"

He grins at me. "Sometimes I think you love him more than you love me."

"Is it that obvious?"

"Yes. Now be a dear and go do host things with our guests."

"Host things? Like what? Help them set up the slip and slide you asked them to bring?"

For a second, I think he's going to try to deny it having been his idea, but he doesn't.

"Yes. I want my turn, dammit."

Shaking my head at him, I round the counter, planting a kiss on his cheek. "You're exhausting."

"I know, but you love it."

"Not more than that apron."

"I doubt that."

"Did you feed your kids this morning?"

He grabs at his chest dramatically. "How dare you insult my competence as the goat-father! Of course I fed my babies. Now out of my kitchen, you evil woman."

"You are something else today. No wonder I'm so worn out."

"Ew, are you two talking about sex?"

I whirl around to find my ex-boyfriend and my best friend standing behind us, their hands clasped together. Zoe's crazy curly hair frames her face, nose upturned at the thought of catching Zach and me talking about sex. Caleb looks unfazed, probably used to the lack of boundaries we all have.

"How'd you two get in here?"

"Turned the handle. Duh."

"So you broke in?"

Zoe lifts a shoulder. "Semantics."

"I told her we should ring the doorbell," Caleb chimes in.

"And I told you that—"

"You do what you want. Yes, I recall that clearly." Caleb's voice sounds flat, like he's heard that reasoning too many times over the years, but his eyes shine with nothing but love.

If you'd have told me back in the day that my best friend and my ex-boyfriend would end up roommates and then fall in love, I'd have straight up told you drugs were bad and you should lay off them.

But here we are, years later, and they're still madly in love.

It's sickening...and I love it.

Caleb is so much like family now that some days I legitimately forget we used to date. Granted, it was only for six months in college, but still, it did happen.

I wasn't even mad when Zoe came to me confessing her feelings for him. How could I be? It was Caleb—he was hard not to fall for with that stupid backward baseball cap of his, the very one he's wearing right now.

"Did you bring ice?" Zach asks, still doing...well, whatever it is he's doing in the kitchen.

To be honest, it looks like he's just pulling random things out of the fridge and putting them back in a different order, but I'm not much of a cook, so what do I know?

"Shit. Be right back." Caleb rushes out the door, headed for the ice I assume he left to melt in the car.

"How are the art classes going?" I ask Zoe, pulling the fridge open as she takes a seat at the bar, tucking her gorgeous sunshine yellow dress under her legs, a habit she's formed since that one time our oldest goat Marshmallow tried to eat her skirt.

"Great. The kids are a hoot. Keep me on my toes, that's for sure, except for that one little brat, Aubrey—so sassy."

"I don't think you're allowed to call the kids at the community center brats, Zoe."

"What?" She cracks open the water bottle I hand her and takes a sip. "I call 'em like I see 'em. Kid is a brat."

She can play tough all she wants, but I know Zoe would do anything for those children.

I thought she was nuts to take on the classes last month on top of her regular workload—running her own gallery full-time—but it turns out it was just what she needed to keep her creativity flowing seamlessly.

Plus, I'm sure it helps that Caleb runs the community center, which means they get to spend a lot more time together, something I'm certain is nice considering he spends a good portion of the year catering to all-star athletes at the local colleges as the top sports nutritionist in the state.

"You're going to make a great mother."

She lays a hand on her stomach, which is barely poking out at sixteen weeks. "Aren't I?"

"Sarcasm, Zoe. That was sarcasm."

"Was it really though?" she tosses back.

"I still can't believe you're pregnant." I slide into the seat next to her, placing my hand beside hers. "She needs to start kicking already. I wanna feel her."

"We don't know if it's a she yet," Zoe chides.

"When do we find out?"

"Next week," Caleb answers, coming back into the kitchen with two bags of ice in hand. "And it's a girl. I know it is."

Zoe lets out a huff. "Stop it, Caleb. You know I don't want to get my hopes up."

"I know, I know, but I'm telling you, I have a feeling. It's a girl."

"I can't wait to meet baby Delia. I hope she has my eyes."

Zoe purses her lips and swats my hand away. "That's not how this works."

"Yeah—if anything, that baby is gonna have *my* eyes."

"That joke would be a lot funnier if you didn't have a wiener, Robbie," Monty says quietly as they enter the kitchen.

Robbie pales when he realizes what just came out of his mouth. "Sex with Zoe." His body is racked with shudders. "Ew."

"Eh." Caleb shrugs. "It's not that bad."

"Not that bad? *Not that bad?!* I am pregnant and hormonal, and you want to say that sex with me is 'not that bad'?"

Zach leans toward the stricken Caleb. "My best advice here, bud? Run."

Caleb takes off as Zoe leaps from the stool, pulling her sandal off as she chases after him. "I will break your balls, Mills!"

"Run, Caleb!" my boyfriend screams. "Run like the wind!"

No one even bats an eye at their antics.

Monty slides into Zoe's abandoned seat. "Thanks for having us over today, Delia."

I point a finger at Zach. "This was all him. If I had my way, I'd be in bed with my boobies hanging free and a crossword puzzle in front of me."

"Delia, stop. Your manners are giving me a boner."

My cheeks heat as I realize how my comment must have sounded. "Shit. I'm sorry, Monty. I didn't mean it like you guys aren't welcome here—you always are. You just know how it goes sometimes when all you wanna do is snuggle in bed and not lift a finger."

"Trust me, I get it. That's me during the school year. Zoe was right—kids can be exhausting."

"Are you two planning on having any of your own?" I ask, and then I cringe at my own question. I loathe it when people try to stick their nose in my business, and here I am doing the same to Monty.

A smile lights her face. "We are."

"We're just practicing right now, but the real trying starts on our wedding night," Robbie explains, bouncing his brows up and down. "Have you two settled on what you want to do about kids yet?"

"We should probably discuss marriage before we jump that far into things, don't ya think?"

Even I hear the bite in my words.

Zach freezes for a moment before he continues shoving things back inside the fridge, pretending I didn't just sound like the biggest bitch in the world.

It's weird when you think about it. Of all the subjects Zach and I have covered in our years together, marriage isn't one of them. Though I've never dreamt of my wedding or anything like that, I always assumed one day my boyfriend of many years would ask, I'd say yes, and the rest would be history.

Nearly five years later, that moment hasn't come, and with every day that passes, I find I want it more and more.

I just don't know if he does too.

I clear my throat. "I mean, no, we haven't really talked about it."

"I'm sure Zach's just waiting for the perfect moment," Monty says quietly, bumping her shoulder into mine. "Unlike his best friend."

"Hey now! I thought the way I proposed was super romantic."

"Yes, Robbie, because it's always been my dream to

be proposed to in the middle of One Hole Donuts over breakfast." Monty rolls her green eyes. "Not."

"Got you to say yes, didn't I?"

Color steals up her cheeks as she mutters, "Fair point."

"You proposed over donuts? How did I not know that? That's romantic as shit!"

"Shit is the least romantic thing in the entire world, Delia."

I pick up the hand towel sitting on the counter and chuck it at my smartass partner. "Shut up, Zachary. You know what I meant."

"Yes, that you think shit is romantic, and *that's* why I haven't proposed yet. We still have some serious work to do with you."

My heart pitter-patters when the word *yet* leaves his lips.

Does that mean he's planning to propose?

Why I am so hung up on this? Ugh! This isn't me. Knock it off, Delia.

"Oh, I heard a yet in there, man! Does that mean you're going to pop the question soon?"

Zach glowers at his best friend. "Shut up and come help me with the grill."

Robbie pretends to zip his lips shut, attempting to

hide a snicker as he follows a scowling Zach out to the back patio.

Caleb's hot on their heels, sliding the door closed as an out-of-breath Zoe claws at the handle, trying to push it back open. She's no match for Caleb's strength, and he wins effortlessly, the big goon not giving his pregnant girlfriend any leeway. He stands at the door, literally patting himself on the back and cheering for being able to lock her out. She slaps at the glass and he begins a victory dance, pressing his denim-clad ass against the door.

Naturally, Zach and Robbie join in, and suddenly there are three asses pressed against the pane.

"Keep shaking that ass, Zach! You're on window-cleaning duty next!"

"Yeah, keep shaking it." Monty stares at the show, hand tucked under her chin, thoroughly enjoying the boys' shenanigans.

Zoe huffs and puffs her way back into the kitchen, pulling the fridge open and grabbing a bottle of water.

"Sure." I wave a hand at her. "Help yourself."

"I will. I'm dying of thirst and you're a terrible host, not offering me anything to drink."

I point to the half-empty bottle sitting on the counter. "Do you not remember drinking half of that?"

"Oops." She shrugs. "Pregnancy brain."

"You can't use that excuse for everything."

"You try having a tiny foreign being sucking all your brain juice from your body 24-7!"

I scrunch my nose. "Ew. Pass."

"You really don't want kids, huh?" Monty observes.

"I really don't."

"You and Zach are so good with Xavie though."

"I know. I love kids...when I can give them back to their parents. We're good playing the fun uncle and cool aunt. We don't need any rug rats of our own. Besides, Zach's enough to deal with, and we have the goats. They're a handful. The last thing we need is a tiny human adding to the mess."

"I get it." She holds her hands up. "Trust me. I think it's kind of cool you're both in agreement over it and know what you want."

I worry my lip between my teeth, hoping and praying Zach and I actually *are* in agreement.

Her mouth drops open when I don't say anything. "You two *have* discussed kids, right?"

"Well, not explicitly."

"You haven't talked marriage *or* kids? How is that possible?"

"How do you know that? You were chasing your baby daddy through the house with your shoe during that conversation."

"My mommy hearing has already kicked in. I heard every word."

I narrow my eyes at her. "Uh huh. You're just being nosy."

"Nosy, concerned—it's all the same."

"Concerned? Why?"

"I dunno, Delia, because marriage and kids are big things to not discuss. Aren't you worried?"

"About?"

"About not wanting the same things. How have you never discussed this before?"

"No. I don't know. They've just never been important to us. I mean, to be fair, we did text for weeks without every knowing basic things about one another like age and job. We don't function the way other couples do."

See? Deep down you know you're solid. You're just a different kind of couple and you're taking it slow.

"*Everyone* talks about marriage and kids, especially when they've been together forever like you two have."

Okay, so maybe you're the wrong kind of different.

"Not us."

"Do you ever worry you don't want the same things and all this time spent with Zach was for nothing?"

"It's not nothing. Zach is..."

My eyes drift toward the backyard, where the three most important grown-ass men in my life are assembling a freaking slip and slide like they're all teenagers and not in their late twenties (or thirties in Zach and Robbie's cases).

He's a complete nut. He does shit he's way too old for and shit he's way too young for. He still wears cartoon underwear for goodness' sake. He's a moron, but he's *my* moron, and no time spent with him is ever wasted.

If he wants kids and I don't, we'll make something work.

If he doesn't want to get married and I do, we'll make something work.

Because that's what we do—we make it work.

We're Zach Hastings and Delia Devlin. We're the duo of all duos. Nothing silly like marriage or kids is going to tear us apart.

I hope.

"Zach isn't nothing, Zoe. He's everything."

She gags. "Spare me. Zach's just a person, and people are replaceable."

"But he's *my* person."

A smile creeps onto her face, because she knows I'm right.

I mean, not about Zach, but I know she understands

because it's the same for her and Caleb. He's her every-thing. They'd make it work too.

Are Zach and I dumb as hell for not talking about our future? Sure, but it doesn't make us any less happy right now, so who cares?

"I can't believe you let those three morons try to man a grill by themselves."

"Can none of you knock?"

Shep, Zach's younger brother, and his wife Denny—who just so happens to be Monty's twin sister—stride into the kitchen, their three-month-old son James sleeping soundly in his baby wrap.

"Where do you want the ice?" Shep holds up a drip-ping bag.

My brows slash together. *Did everyone bring ice?*

"Is that a real question, dingus?" Denny sighs. "The freezer, obviously."

"Right, that makes sense. Sorry," Shep mutters, making his way over. "Sleep deprivation and all that."

It's an excuse I'll allow, because baby James has colic and I know the two of them are exhausted. Zach and I offered to take his nephew for a night last week and we slept a total of three hours...between the two of us.

It was a nightmare.

"How's he doing?" I nod toward the sleeping angel.

Denny covers the baby's ears. "Okay so far today.

Sorry, gotta cover them so he doesn't hear and then decide to not be so okay. I love the little guy, but I also love and miss sleep desperately. I wouldn't wish this upon my worst enemy."

"No, just random strangers at the Smart Shoppe." Shep presses a kiss to his son's head, and Denny swats at him, not wanting him to wake the baby.

"Denver Andrews!" Monty admonishes, and Denny glares at her for using the wrong last name. "Clark, whatever. I'm still getting used to it. You cannot be rude to strangers just because *you're* tired. Our momma raised you better than that."

Denny points to her son. "You try having this demon scream at all hours of the day and then once you finally lull him to sleep with the soothing movement of the cart, an old hag crashes into you with her freakin' electric scooter, waking your baby up and *refusing* to apologize. Then talk to me about how our momma raised us."

"You should have seen her." Shep's eyes widen at the memory. "She was angrier than when she was trying to push the demon out."

"Don't call our baby a demon!"

"You *just* called him that yourself!"

"32 hours of labor," she reminds him. "I can call him whatever I want. Right now he's an angel—*my* angel."

She gazes down, pressing soft kisses to said angel's head. "Isn't that right, Bucky Jr? You're Momma's little Winter Solider, huh?" she coos.

"See, it would have been a good name," Shep mutters bravely.

Denny glares him. "Stop talking."

He smooshes his lips together, trying his hardest not to laugh at his exhausted wife. "Yes ma'am."

"Ugh. Go somewhere else before I maim you."

A laugh bubbles out of him, but he's smart enough to move out of her reach, heading toward the back patio to join the other meatheads.

"'Sup, nerds?" he says, pushing open the door. "The hot one has arrived."

They all groan—rightfully so—then Zach hands him a beer.

I smile at the interaction.

Despite growing up close, there was once a time when Zach and Shep pretended the other didn't exist. I mean, it was completely justified, what with Shep sending a nude photo of me out to all his baseball friends. It's taken a lot of effort from all parties involved, but we've moved on and have forgiven him for his past mistakes.

When Shep and Denny found out they were pregnant shortly after they began dating, they ran off to Vegas and got hitched without telling anyone.

A month later, they lost the baby. Shep needed his brother, and despite Zach still being angry, he was there for him through it all. With time—and a few fistfights—the boys rebuilt their relationship from scratch, and things between Shep and me fell into a natural rhythm as a result. We're not tight by any means, but I don't hate him anymore.

Besides, he gave me an adorable little nephew to fawn over. I can't stay mad at him forever, not when James is so perfect...you know, despite the colic and not letting me sleep thing.

"I want to strangle him, but I love that idiot," Denny says dreamily, leaning against the counter, adjusting James on her chest. She grimaces at the shuffling. "God, my back is killing me."

"Oh goodness, where are my manners?" Monty pushes up from the stool. "Here, take my seat, Denny."

"No, I'm good. If I sit, I sleep, and I don't want to miss the big party today."

"Big party?" I laugh. "It's just a barbeque. We don't mind if you sleep."

"I'm fine. Promise. Sit back down, Monty."

Monty points between the chair and Zoe, and Zoe shakes her head.

"I'm good. It's kind of uncomfortable to sit on those things."

Denny points to James. "Trust me, sit now while you can."

Zoe laughs. "If you change your mind and want to nap and take advantage of free babysitting, I'll take him. I could use the practice."

"We'll see how I'm feeling in a few hours." Denny yawns. "I might take you up on that. By the way, before I forget, Allie and AJ wanted me to extend their gratitude for the invite, but they won't be making it. They're in fucking Belize for the week."

"Belize? Good lord. How is that even possible?"

"Shep."

"I wish my best friend would pay for my vacation." Zoe crosses her arms over her chest, pouting my way.

Denny chuckles. "No, for *signing* Shep to his team for the next three years. He's making waves as his new agent. They're loving working together."

"I still can't believe Shep went into that deal with him." Zoe shakes her head. Caleb and AJ spend a lot of time together at the community center, AJ helping run it when he's not off signing multi-million dollar contracts, apparently. "AJ's greener than green, and those idiots managed to make the deal of the century."

"Hey." Denny shrugs. "He almost talked his high

school girlfriend into marrying him...while still in high school. Dude has major moves."

"I'll give you that, but still."

"Does this mean we get free tickets to the games?"

"Montana! You greedy little snake!"

"What?" Monty blinks innocently. "Baseball pants are hot."

"I'm so telling Robbie you said that."

"Go for it." She lifts a shoulder. "He'll just go out and buy some then rope me into some weird roleplay."

"Roleplay? Spill!"

I push away from the stool, plugging my ears. "Nope. No. Robbie's like a brother. I don't wanna hear it. I'm gonna go check on the morons."

CHAPTER 3

"DUDE, I'm telling you, just dump some beer on it. We'll slide down so fast it'll make your head spin."

"No, no." Caleb shakes his head, disagreeing with Robbie. "We need water. The beer is just going to make it sticky."

"But the beer will also make it taste better."

"Why the hell are you drinking the water?" Zach asks, pushing those sexy-as-fuck glasses up his sharp nose. "What if someone farts on their way down? You'll be drinking their fart water."

And there goes his sexiness factor, right out the window.

"I swear to god, if anyone farts and ruins this slip and slide, I'll punch you all," Shep vows.

"You can't command us not to fart. That's not how assholes work."

I blink twice at the scene in front me, listening to these dumbasses talk about farts.

The shirts have come off and two empty beer bottles sit by the cooler as Shep and Caleb work to get the slip and slide set up. Robbie's trying to get the hose to work. Zach's standing in front of the grill, still wearing his apron over his chest—which, for some reason, is now shirtless—spatula in hand as he watches the scene play out in front of him.

I have no idea what's going on.

"I can't believe any of you are in relationships."

"Even me?" Zach grins, spinning toward me, sauntering my way and wrapping an arm around my waist.

"Especially you, Mr. Fart Water!"

"Ha ha. She thinks you're dumb." Robbie tries to spray his best friend with the hose, and when it doesn't work, he turns it on himself, dousing his own face.

"Don't worry, I think you're dumb too." I wink at him.

"What's up?" Zach shuffles the aluminum pan sitting on the side table attached to the grill. *Huh.* He must have brought that out before I came downstairs. "Need something?"

"Just came to make sure you boys didn't need help with anything, but I can see you have it all under control out here."

"Yep. Plenty of fart-free water for the slip and slide, got the meat frying, and all that fun stuff."

"Frying?" I give him a *what the fuck* look. "It's called grilling. Even I know that."

"Right, grilling. Whatever. Same-same diff."

"Yeah, Delia. Same-same diff," Robbie echoes.

I groan at the saying, having heard it way too many times over the years. "Remind me again why you decided to have a barbeque and invite people over?"

"Because you love us," Caleb offers.

"I love one of you."

He gives me a cocky grin. "It's me, isn't it?"

"Are you forgetting she dumped you? It's definitely not you, dude." Robbie shakes his head then puffs his chest out. "It's clearly me. I'm the handsomest."

"Not that I'm throwing my hat into the ring or anything because we all know I'm a dick—and *have* the biggest dick, just so we're clear—but I want to clarify that *I'm* the handsomest." Shep shoots me wink. "We all know it too."

"How many beers have you idiots had? Clearly she loves *me* the most." Zach smiles smugly. "Right, baby?"

"I have no idea why you're all debating this. I obviously meant Marshmallow."

"Gasp! And leave out Graham Cracker and Milk Chocolate? You're a terrible goat mom."

"What can I say? Marshy stole my heart first."

"Before me?" Zach presses.

"*Especially* before you," I tease.

"I'd pretend to be offended, but I can't blame you one bit. He *is* adorable."

"Indeed. But can you tell me why our goat is wearing a bowtie?"

I feel Zach stiffen for only a moment before he relaxes and throws me a grin. "Because he's minding his own business."

"Right. None of my business."

I look out at the scene in front of me: three of the best guys I've ever met, trying to get a slip and slide operational.

Idiots.

"We did a good job with them, you know."

"The goats?"

Zach chuckles softly. "Them too, but I was talking about the guys. Can you believe they're all so...grown up? I mean, Caleb's going to be a dad. Robbie's getting married. Shep's married *and* has a kid. It's crazy how far they've all come."

Grown up. Those two words stick out for me. Is that how he sees them, as grown up? And because of marriages and babies?

Then where does that leave us? Are we just two kids

playing house?

"Crazy," I say quietly.

"Hey." He shakes me. "Everything okay?"

No. I think I want to marry you, but I don't know if you want to marry me and I'm way too chickenshit to say anything about it and the last thing I'm going to do is bring it up in front of our friends.

"Yeah, of course." I smile. "Everything's great."

His eyes bore into me, like he's trying to read me, and my heart rate picks up. It's hammering so hard, I'm certain he can hear it, and I'm not ready for a serious conversation right now.

Shit shit shit.

After what feels like hours under his heated gaze, his lips stretch wide into a smile and he pecks a kiss to my forehead. "Just checking. You ladies doing okay in there? Hot dogs will be done in a bit."

"Hot dogs?" Now it's my turn to eye him because I am almost certain he told me he was making burgers.

"H-Hot dogs? No, no. I meant burgers." He smiles, but his lips waver. "My bad."

"Right. Did you happen to plan out this barbeque of yours at all? Buy any snacks for appetizers? I have a pregnant chick in there, you know. We can't go without provisions for too long unless you want one of us girls to eat the other." Before a comment can be made, I throw my hand up and slide my eyes toward the lawn. "I swear to god, Robert, if you make one joke about eating pussy, I will twist your nuts off."

Robbie snaps his mouth closed, and Caleb snickers at the reprimand before I turn my fiery gaze to him. His back goes ramrod straight and he sobers up, averting his eyes like the smart man he is.

"Snacks are in the cabinet next to the right of the fridge," he tells me.

"I snuck out of the house this morning while you were napping and grabbed everything we'd need."

My mouth drops. "You knew I was napping the whole time?"

"Yeah. Why else would I leave you alone for two whole hours? Because I'm nice? No way. You know I get bored too easily and would want attention."

I press a kiss to his lips. "Exhausting," I whisper against his mouth.

He tightens his grip on me, smashing my body tight against his. "You said that last night too."

Shoving at his chest, I laugh at his attempt to show off in front of the guys. "We didn't even bang last night."

"We did in my dreams, baby."

"I'm going back inside before I make you start digging your own grave."

"You'd make him dig his own grave? Damn, girl. I

like your style," Shep says, impressed.

"Just make sure your kids are in their house before you start slipping and sliding all over the yard," I remind him, pulling open the door and giving my hips an extra shake because I know he's watching me.

He gives a low whistle, and I slide the door closed, laughing at the dork.

Maybe we haven't lost our spark at all.

"SIXTY MINUTES! PAY UP!"

Groaning, I push off the couch, grabbing my purse from the console next to the front door and pulling out a twenty.

The girls were all lounging in the living room when I came back inside, watching the boys act like morons. Naturally, a bet was placed. I was team broken bone within the hour, while Denny gave them the benefit of the doubt.

I lost.

"Lucky brat," I grumble, sliding the bill into her waiting hand. "Watch, it'll happen within the next ten minutes now."

"Wanna bet?" Denny winks, and I stick my

tongue out.

I toss my purse back onto the table and reclaim my comfy spot on the couch.

Zoe nods toward the backyard. "What's on the menu for this shindig?" She rubs at her growing belly. "Someone's hungry."

"Burgers—or maybe hot dogs. Even Zach's not sure."

"Not sure as in he can't tell them apart? Because if that's the case, we need to have a chat, and not with him. I mean with you, 'cause your boy is dumb as hell."

"I don't know what's up with him. I was hoping for a lazy day—no offense to any of you ladies—but here we are hosting a barbeque I knew absolutely nothing about."

I glance out back, my brows pulling together when I see Zach staring down at his phone...again. I try not to be frustrated, but it's hard.

"He's been so...off lately."

"Is everything okay with you two?" Monty asks, picking up on the lingering sadness in my voice.

"Of course!" My response is too quick. "I mean... yeah. We're good."

She doesn't press, but she doesn't have to. I can see in her eyes she doesn't believe me.

I don't know if I believe me either.

I shoot up from the couch, annoyed with myself for

thinking that way. "I'm grabbing wine. Anyone want wine? Let's have wine."

Though I can feel tears brimming in my eyes, I casually make my way into the kitchen and away from the curious stares my friends are sending me.

Fumbling my way through the blurriness, I pull the fridge open and take out a fresh bottle of wine.

I unscrew the top—because let's be honest, I'm no fancy bitch—and grab two glasses from the cabinet.

"Hey."

"AH!"

The wine goes tumbling to the floor, the sound of broken glass echoing. The white liquid soaks my jeans and seeps between my toes, and I'm more annoyed my socks are wet than I am about the spilled wine.

"Dammit, Zoe!"

"Shit! I am so sorry, Delia." She rushes toward me, but I hold my hand out.

"Stop! Glass."

"Then step away so I can hug you!"

"What's wrong? What happened?" Monty comes running into the room, Denver hot on her heels. She gasps at the sight before her. "Oh my cats! Delia, get away from there before you cut yourself. Denny, grab me the broom. Zoe, go away. You're pregnant."

Zoe huffs but takes a few steps back. "I'm pregnant,

not broken...unlike the bottle Mrs. Butterfingers here just let drop."

"Because you scared me! You're lucky I didn't shit myself!"

"Girls don't poop," Monty insists quietly.

"You must be real full of shit then," Denny says, handing the broom to her sister.

Monty throws her a look. "Just grab me some towels."

"Damn. You're bossy like your fiancé."

I try to stay calm, but the word fiancé sets off the waterworks, and before I know it, I'm enveloped by Zoe's warm embrace.

By some miracle, nobody says anything about dramatics. Instead, Zoe silently ushers me upstairs into my bedroom.

The door clicks closed behind us as she leads me to the bed, pushing at my shoulders until I'm sitting.

I stay wrapped in her arms, crying until there's nothing left inside me.

Sniffling, I eventually push away from her, swiping at the hot tears staining my cheeks.

"God." I push out a heavy breath. "I'm a mess."

"You are." She pauses for a moment. "Delia?"

"Yeah?"

"You're pregnant, aren't you?"

CHAPTER 4

"GOD, NO!"

She tilts her head, eyeing me and obviously not believing me. "Are you sure?"

"Yes!" I sigh. "I swear. I took a test last week and it was negative."

"Then why are you such an emotional wreck lately? I have never seen you like you this before. You're starting to worry me."

My chin wobbles and more tears threaten to fall from my eyes, but I blink them away, holding on to my last shred of dignity. She's right; I'm not usually like this. I'm generally pretty damn good at holding myself together, but at the moment I feel like I'm falling apart at the seams.

"I don't know. I think it's just my hormones or something."

"But definitely not pregnant?"

"Zoe!"

She holds her hands up. "Fine, fine. Not pregnant—got it." She bumps her shoulder with mine. "Wanna talk about it?"

"I don't know…" I sigh. "I probably should."

"Then talk." She pushes off the bed. "Lie back. Close your eyes. I'll grab you new clothes, you talk. That way you don't feel like I'm just staring at you. Maybe you'll open up more."

"That's dumb."

Glaring, she points a finger at me. "Just do what I say."

"You're getting a little too into this whole mommy-tude thing already."

"Shut up." She shoves at my shoulders. "Back."

I fall backward, letting myself sink into the comfy bed, exhaling deeply.

I listen as my best friend shuffles around my closet, letting everything inside me simmer.

She's right—I do need to talk about it—but I'm right too. This is dumb. I'm being dumb.

But what if I'm not?

"I-I…" Another deep breath. "I think Zach might be over me."

Zoe lets out a snort. "Right."

"I'm serious, Zoe."

"No you're not. That's the hormones talking."

"Maybe...maybe not. Maybe it's a five-year relationship that's going nowhere. Maybe it's the fact that he'd rather be on his phone working than spend time with me. Maybe it's that instead of lounging in bed all day long, he'd rather invite our friends over for a stupid barbeque when he hardly even knows how to work a grill. Maybe it's the fact that we haven't had sex in three weeks, or that he doesn't kiss me as passionately as he used to. Maybe, just maybe, he's bored of me."

When she doesn't respond, I rise up on my elbows, searching her out.

My mouth drops open when I find her doubled over in laughter.

I don't care if she's pregnant or not—I reach for the nearest pillow and chuck it at her with all my might.

She's lucky I'm a bad shot, the pillow landing at least a foot to the left.

"Stop laughing!"

Another guffaw. "I can't."

"Zoe!"

"Maybe, just maybe, you're being a dumbass."

"You are the worst!"

"What! I'm just being honest. You're being dumb."

I push off the bed and head toward the door, but she beats me there, blocking my exit.

"Move."

"No. Not until we talk about this more."

I glare.

She takes the brunt of my heated stare, not budging.

"Fine." I retreat to the bed. "But stop laughing."

"I'll stop laughing when you stop making mountains out of donut holes."

"Donut holes?"

She lifts a slender shoulder. "What? I'm hungry. Just go with it."

When she trusts I'm not going to flee, she returns to the closet, flicking through the blouses and dresses hanging in an orderly fashion.

"I say this with all the love in the world, Delia, but you're stupid as fuck."

"You're right. I can definitely feel the love."

"I'm serious. I love you, you know that, but nobody in this world—not even your mother—loves you more than Zach does, and I'm kind of annoyed with you for even questioning that."

"Then why does it feel like we're drifting apart? Why aren't we having sex? Why does it sometimes feel like we're going nowhere?"

"The no-sex thing is totally normal. You're not always going to paw at each other like you did when you first started dating."

"Do you and Caleb still bang like bunnies?"

"Hell no." She snorts. "Sometimes I want to touch him constantly. Sometimes I don't even want to hear him breathe. It's all about balance. And as for going nowhere...you're not going nowhere. Trust me."

She says it like she's never been more sure of anything in her life, and I'm so annoyed I can't be that certain of my own relationship.

The stupid tears I've barely been holding back fall, and I rush to clean them off before she can see them.

Like she has a sixth sense or something, Zoe spins my way, giving me a single glance before rushing to my side. Her own chin wobbles, and she's crying too.

The thing is, she has that whole bun-in-the-oven reason for being emotional. Me? I'm just a basket case.

She wraps an arm around me, pulling me into her.

"I need you to stop crying. I'm not emotionally equipped to see you in tears right now. If you cry, I cry, and I really fucking hate crying."

Laughing, I lift my shirt and wipe the tears, not caring about the stain I'll have from my mascara.

"How do you know?"

"That Zach loves you?"

"Yeah. I mean, how do *you* know and I don't?"

"You know he loves you. Don't pretend otherwise.

You're just using this whole 'he doesn't love me' bit as a coping mechanism."

"For?"

She puffs out a breath. "Look, I get it—you wanna be Kelly Clarkson circa 2003, Miss Independent and all that shit. You don't *want* to want the fairytale happily ever after. You've never been that girl, but face it—your friends are all getting theirs and dammit you want one too. It's natural." She chucks my chin. "It's *okay* to want something more."

"H-How did you..."

"Know?" A shrug. "Because you're my best friend, Delia—that and I saw how you reacted when Robbie and Monty announced their engagement. You had this spark in your eye that said, *I want that*, and then you glared at Zach the rest of the night."

I gasp. "I did not!"

She nods. "Afraid so."

"Well, shit."

Laughing, she stands and heads for the closet yet again. She pulls down Zach's favorite dress—okay, fine, it's my favorite—and walks it over to me.

"Here, put this on."

"What? Don't you think it's a bit fancy for a barbeque?"

"When you feel like shit but look like gold, you're gold, baby."

Chuckling, I grab the dress. "Fair enough."

I stand, stripping down to my unders. Zoe, more than used to my nudity since we lived together once upon a time, doesn't bat an eye.

She takes a seat, crossing her legs and pecking away on her phone—probably reassuring Denny and Monty I'm okay—while I head into the bathroom to straighten myself out.

I fix the minimal amount of makeup I had on and pull my hair from my messy bun. Twisting it into a side braid, I try not to overthink everything...again.

"Hey Zoe?"

"Yeah?"

"Do you think I'm stupid for wanting to marry Zach?"

"Are you serious? I'm surprised as shit you two didn't do what Shep and Denny did and run off to Vegas shortly after you agreed to move in with him. You and Zach were made for each other, Delia. Nothing is going to come between you."

"What if he doesn't want to marry me?"

"I don't think that's something you need to worry about."

Pausing mid-twist, I poke my head into the

bedroom, eyeing her. "Why do you sound so certain about that? Has he said something to you? To Caleb?"

"No, dumbass." She taps the side of her head. "I'm just using logic instead of my emotions."

"Shut up," I mutter, returning my attention to the task at hand.

"Here's a genius idea: why don't you, *I dunno*, talk to your boyfriend about it?"

"It's hard."

"That's what she said."

"Zoe!"

"What?" she says with innocence. "You walked right into that one."

"I'm being serious."

"I am too. Right into it."

"No, I mean about it being hard. I know it sounds easier to just talk to him instead of agonizing over it, but talking about it is...awkward. I don't want to sound desperate for validation by bringing it up."

"Honey, you're dating him. He already knows you're desperate."

I ignore her. "How do you tell someone you love them but you want more?"

"Just spitballing here, but have you tried *I love you, but I want more?*"

I roll my eyes, walking out into the bedroom. "Remind me why I'm friends with you again?"

"Because I was the one who told you to put that dress on and you look fabulous in it."

"Oh, is that why?" I twirl. "I do look great."

"Do you feel any better?"

"A little, but I still want to talk to him."

"So do it. Talk to him. It's simpler than you're making it."

Talk to him.

She's right. I *should* talk to him.

Bravery inflates me, and I have the sudden urge to barge down those stairs and tell Zach exactly how I feel. I know myself well enough to know if I don't take advantage of the sudden flood of courage, I'll lose it.

"Zoe?"

She doesn't look up from her phone. "That's me."

"I'm gonna talk to him."

"Uh-huh."

"No, Zoe." She finally shifts her eyes my way. "I'm *gonna* talk to him."

"Good. You should."

"I am going to talk to him—right now."

Her eyes widen. "Like *now* now?"

"Yep, because if I don't, I'll chicken out."

I march toward the door, adrenaline surging through my veins.

"*Now* now?" she shrieks, charging off the bed after me.

"Yes, dammit!"

"With all our friends here?"

"Yep!"

I race down the stairs, bypassing Monty and Denny, who sit there stunned, probably confused as hell.

I fling open the back door, scaring Shep and Caleb, who are relaxing on the patio as Robbie and Zach race down the slide.

"What's going on?" Denny asks as she and Monty join us outside.

"Hey, Hastings!" I yell out across the lawn.

Zach catches himself mid-slide, dark hair dripping, water sliding down his cut body, and turns his attention fully on me.

"Yeah, Devlin?"

"I wanna marry you!"

CHAPTER 5

"ALL RIGHT. Which one of you shits told her?"

They all shake their heads.

"Told me what?" I ask.

"Come on. Was it you, Zoe? You suck at secrets."

"Hey, take that back!" She points at him angrily, looking every bit the mama bear she's soon to become. "I didn't say shit!"

"Robbie?" Zach accuses.

He holds his hands up. "No way, bro. I know better."

"All right, then who?"

I march toward him, not stopping until I'm a foot away, hands on my hips. I peer up into his captivating green eyes, my toes tapping against the grass.

"Told me what, Zachary?"

"What today is."

"An impromptu cookout?"

His brows draw together as he stares down at me, tongue darting out to catch the water dripping down his face. He's watching me closely, looking for any sign I'm messing with him.

I'm not.

"You really don't know?"

"No, dammit!" I stamp my foot, annoyed, because I'm clearly missing out on something big. "Just tell me what's going on."

"Your wedding!"

My hand flies to my chest and a sharp gasp rushes from my lungs.

"M-My w-what?"

He sighs, running a hand over his face. "This isn't how it was supposed to go, but fuck it."

The last thing I was ever expecting happens before my eyes.

Zach drops to one knee, and my heart drops right along with him. He looks up at me with a shy grin, something I'm not used to from him.

"Delia Devlin, will you marry me?"

I'm frozen.

Completely shocked.

I stand there, mouth hanging open, staring down at the man of my dreams...just blinking.

I don't know how much time passes, but it's long enough for Zach's smile to begin to waver.

"Delia?" he says, speaking quietly so only I can hear him. "Did you hear me?"

Something snaps inside me, and the next thing I know, I'm swatting at him.

"Ouch! Hey! Watch it!" He pushes to his feet, moving away from my assault. "Is that a no?"

"You stubborn asshole!" I whack him again. "I swear to god, Zachary..."

"I'm starting to think it's a no."

"You made me sit around waiting for *five fucking years* for you to try to *surprise* me with my own wedding day? Are you shitting me?"

"N-No?"

"OH MY GOD!" I pinch his nipple between my thumb and forefinger, twisting it hard. "PURPLE NURPLE!"

"JESUS DELIA!" He wrenches himself out of my grip. "This is the worst proposal ever!"

"You're telling me, you ass! I cannot believe you right now!"

"Are you saying yes or no?"

"YES!" I screech. "You know it's yes."

"This is so weird," I hear Robbie say.

Zach and I yell at the same time, "Shut up, Robbie!"

Caleb snickers, and we both glare at him. He whistles, taking a sip of beer, averting his gaze.

"What the hell were you thinking, Zach?"

"That I love you?"

"I'm serious!"

"I am too, Delia. I love the shit out of you."

"Shit is the least romantic thing in the entire world, Zach," I shoot back, echoing his words from earlier. "Why now, huh? After all this time?"

He grins, and I know he wants to call me on my unintentional Harry Potter reference, but he knows better than to do so in the middle of a conversation this serious.

"Honestly?"

"No. Lie to me," I smart off.

He ignores me. "It was that night in the restaurant when dipshit over there"—he points to Robbie—"beat me to the punch and announced that he'd proposed to Monty. Something inside me clicked and I thought, *That should be us.*"

He grabs my hands, trapping them in his own, and tugs me closer. My breath catches, heart racing so hard I'm almost afraid I'm going to have a heart attack right here in front of everyone.

I know they're all staring, but right now it feels as if it's just the two of us.

"Look," he starts, his voice a whisper. "I know we haven't really talked about marriage. I honestly never knew if you wanted it or not and I didn't want to pressure you, but I do, Delia. I want it. I want to marry you so badly. I want to call you Delia Hastings. I want to call you wife. I want to call you *mine*."

Tears drip down my cheeks, this time for a good reason.

"Hey, don't cry." The pad of Zach's thumb feels rough across my face. "That's not allowed."

"I can't help it. I'm just so...happy. I've been wanting to talk to you about marriage for *weeks*."

"So why didn't you?"

"I was scared."

"Of what?"

"You turning me down."

He scoffs. "Please. Like that's possible. I mean, have you *seen* your ass?"

I laugh. "You really planned a whole wedding for today? Just assumed I was going to say yes?"

"There was never a doubt in my mind you'd say anything else."

"How could you be so sure?"

"Because, Delia, you're it for me. And besides..." He drops his lips to my ear. "Dimples."

Laughter bubbles out of me. "I can't believe you."

"Believe it, baby."

"Are we really getting married today?"

"If you want to, yes. I've kind of been planning it for weeks now. It's why I've been on my phone constantly, making sure everything was in order."

Ah, that explains so much.

"Is that why Marshmallow's wearing a bowtie?"

"What? No, that's dumb. He just looks cute in it."

My lips twitch because, to Zach, a goat in a bowtie makes perfect sense, but not if it's for a wedding.

"I'm not dressed for a wedding, you know."

He glances down at my dress. "You're wearing your ranch dressing bottle dress. I couldn't imagine you in anything else."

"*You're* not dressed for a wedding."

"Fine." He rolls his eyes. "I'll put my Ryan Reynolds apron back on. Stop begging."

"I didn't wash my hair today."

"You act like that's something new." He tugs me closer, wrapping his arms around me, neither of us caring about how wet he is. "Now, any other trivial excuse you got?"

"No."

"Good, because I *really* wanna marry you today, Delia."

His lips find mine, and for the first time in a while, everything feels right.

"Hey! Knock it off. We aren't at that part yet," Robbie hollers. "Zoe, let's do this shit!"

"She was in on it?"

"Yep."

"Was everyone in on it?"

Denny raises her hand. "I'm surprised as hell right now."

"What she said," Monty agrees. "I'm also annoyed-slash-impressed that Robert kept it a secret."

"I'm sorry, babe," he says to her. "I'll make sure to dick you real good later to make up for it."

Monty's cheeks flame red, and everyone groans at his crassness. In typical Robbie fashion, he doesn't care.

Zoe comes running back out of the house, tossing her phone at Caleb. "Here, record this shit for their parents. I gotta go be maid of honor." She runs down to where we're standing, wrapping her arms around my neck, squeezing me. "Surprise! Happy wedding day!"

I hold her tightly. "I'm going to kill you later."

"No you're not. I'm bearing your godchild."

"Fine, but after Baby Delia's here, you're dead."

Pulling away, she laughs. "Deal." She claps her hands together. "Okay, here we go!"

Robbie steps up to Zach, acting as the witness.

"Uh, aren't we missing an officiant?"

"Oh, right. How could I forget?" Zach shakes his head. "Hey! Anyone here happen to be an officiant?"

Caleb rises from his chair. "Well, shit. I just happened to get certified last night. What a coincidence."

"What!" Zoe cries. "You're in on this too?"

"You aren't the only sneaky one." He winks at her and hands her phone off to Shep. "You just got promoted to videographer. Zoe, quit hollering. You're gonna scare the baby."

She grabs her sandal off her foot, shaking it at him.

Caleb actually flinches.

"Look," Zach says, "this isn't like *official* official because we don't have marriage certificate yet. I tried getting one, but they thought I was kidnapping you and forcing you into marriage or some shit, but we can go right after this, get the certificate, sign it, and we're good to go, or we can go now. Up to you."

"I want to marry you *right now*."

Zach takes my hands, squeezing them. "Good, because I can't wait another second."

"Then shut up so I can officiate this thing." Caleb slides a sheet of paper from his pocket and clears his throat. "It all started with a strapping young lad getting dumped by his hot—but not hotter than his baby momma—ex-girlfriend."

"Caleb!" Zoe seethes.

"Right, right. I'll skip ahead." He stares at the paper for a second before folding it and tucking it away. "You know, I had this whole romantic speech planned, but I think I'm gonna scrap it, and not just because Zoe would have my balls if I continued. We're here today to celebrate two people who are the epitome of unconditional love. There's nothing traditional about Zach and Delia, especially given their meet cute. I mean, who keeps texting the wrong number and gets the girl in the end? Hastings, that's who. Who buys a baby goat for a stranger? Hastings. Who invites everyone over for a wedding masked as a barbeque and then doesn't serve any barbeque? Hastings. Spoiler alert: he ordered pizzas."

"With extra ranch," my soon-to-be husband interjects. "You're all welcome."

Caleb points at him. "Remember what I said about unconditional? That right there is proof of it, because there are a whole lot of conditions attached to what he just said. Really, man? Ranch and pizza?"

Zach shrugs. "Don't knock it until you try it."

"Never. Ranch is the devil's semen."

"Caleb Mills! You cannot say semen during a wedding ceremony!"

"Ah, shit. I forgot we were still doing that." Everyone laughs. "Right. *Ahem.* Anyway, I'd go through the whole *if anyone has anything to say do it now* speech, but no one here is going to object. I mean, how could you?" Caleb smiles warmly at us. "Delia, I love you like a sister, and I am so happy you found someone brave enough to take you on."

Tears prick my eyes and I smile, trying to fight them. "Thank you, Caleb."

"Hastings? Does she let you have half the pizza?"

"She does."

"Then you're definitely the one."

Zach laughs.

"Okay, as we can all see, I am clearly very bad at this, and believe it or not, my script was worse, but let's be honest—this wedding wouldn't be a Zach and Delia event without a little awkwardness. So, let's get to the important part." Caleb faces me. "Delia Devlin, do you take Zach Hastings to be your awfully wedded husband?"

"Lawfully." Zoe sighs. "I cannot believe I let you get me pregnant."

"Can I just ask one question first?"

Zach furrows his brows. "Like right now?"

"Yes. It's important."

"Shoot."

"How do you feel about kids?"

"Ew!" He shudders. "I mean, they're great when I can give them back to their parents, but I'll pass on having my own. Besides, we have our hands full with the goats...and me."

He winks, and I laugh.

"Then I do."

"Zachary Hastings, do take Delia Devlin to be your *awfully*"—he smirks a little—"wedded wife?"

"Send it."

"Zachary! That is not I do!" I admonish.

"Same-same diff, Delia," Robbie chimes in. "Just kiss this dumbass already. It's my turn for the slip and slide."

"This is the weirdest wedding I've ever attended," Denny says.

"If it makes you feel any better, I'm recording it on two phones so we can watch all this awkwardness from multiple angles later," Shep tells her.

Denny points to her sister. "Make sure you get your sister-in-law boohooing over there."

Shep turns the cameras toward Monty, who hides her face behind her hands.

"Stop! I can't help it. It's just so beautiful!"

"Who has the rings?" Caleb asks.

"Funny story about that..." Robbie rocks back on his heels. "I was hiding Zach's ring in my pocket and it fell out." He winces. "Then Milk Chocolate kind of ate it. So, we're gonna have to do rings later...like maybe tomorrow."

"We should really submit this to Sundance," Shep suggests.

"If we don't win a fucking Oscar for this shit, I'm gonna be so pissed," Denny agrees.

"Right." Caleb presses forward. "Rings later. Well, then, by the power vested in me by Help I Need to Officiate My Friend's Wedding dot com, I now pronounce you husband and wife. You may now kiss the bride, but make it fast, because the pizza's getting cold."

My eyes meet Zach's, and there's nothing but that unconditional love Caleb mentioned shining in them. He leans into me, smiling, those dimples I fell in love with poking through.

"What do you say, Delia?" he whispers, our lips so close but not quite touching. "You jump..."

This moment? It's my favorite moment of my entire life.

"I jump."

And we take the leap together.

Want more Zach & Delia?

Here's a cute little Valentine's Day short I wrote.
This short scene takes place after *Let's Get Textual* and
before *Textin' Up My Heart*.

LET'S GET IT* ON
*VALENTINE'S DAY

ZACH

"Zach, you about ready?"

"Coming!"

I hit save on the snippet of code I'm working on and put my laptop to sleep before closing the lid. I have this weird obsession where I always put my computer to sleep when I'm not staring at it. It needs some shuteye too, right?

After slipping my feet into my shoes, grabbing my jacket and keys off the chair, and head to the stairs to meet up with my hopefully soon-to-be ex-roommate, Robbie.

I'm not an ass (most of the time), but I say *hopefully soon-to-be* because tonight, on Valentine's Day, I'm asking my girlfriend Delia to move in with me.

We haven't been together that long yet, less than six months, but you know what they say: when you know, you know.

And I definitely fucking know.

This girl came crashing into my world last year via a wrong number and I haven't been able to get her off my mind since. We have so much and nothing in common all at once. She's become my person in such a short amount of time, and I can't see her never being in my life.

Add in all the bullshit we've already had to endure thanks to my jackass stepbrother, who I'm still not speaking to, I know we're ready.

We're *solid*.

"Zaaaach," Robbie draws my name out in annoyance from the top of the stairs.

"Yeah, yeah. I'm coming. Hold on to your Barbie panties."

"They are not Barbie. They're Bratz dolls."

"You're joking..."

"Am I?"

With Robbie? Who knows.

Shaking my head, I climb the stairs to the main level of the house.

Making my way into the living room, Robbie on my heels, I peer out the bay windows, checking on my baby goats Marshmallow, Graham Cracker, and Milk Chocolate and making sure they're secure in the house I built for them before locking up.

We climb into my car and begin our trek across town. We're about five miles down the road before Robbie speaks again.

"Are you sure she's ready to move in? That's a huge step. What if Delia says no?"

I chuckle and run a hand down my chest. "Please, like she could say no to all of this."

I don't even have to be looking at Robbie to know he rolls his eyes.

"Many girls would say no to all of *that*."

"But not Delia," I argue.

"*Maybe* not Delia."

"No. No *maybe* bullshit. Think positive, Robbie."

"Why? So I can be kicked out of my house?"

"You're not being kicked out. You could totally still live with us if you want."

"And have to hear, '*Oh, please, Professor McGonagall, let me into your Chamber of Secrets.*'" He shudders. "Which is really fucking gross because McGonagall is old as shit, man. Do you *really* wanna slide all up into that dried up Chamber of Secrets?"

"One, it's called roleplay. McGonagall is young in our fantasies. Two, you *listen* to us?"

"You act like I have a choice. Do you have any idea how loud you two can get?"

I smirk because I *do* know. It's loud. "Don't you own headphones or something?"

"So now I have to wear headphones in my own home while you go to Nerd Funkytown with your lady? No way, bro."

"Creep."

He rolls his eyes again and mutters, "Whatever."

"Robbie, man, I want to be sure you're okay with this before I go through with it. You're my main man and I don't want to cause any trouble between us."

He twists his face up. "Shut the hell up, dude. If I had a problem, I wouldn't beat around the bush with it. I'd let you know. I'm just giving you shit. We're good. I'll never repeat this sappy trash again, but I admire the relationship you and Delia have built. I think you're good for each other on many levels and I know you're going to make it the long haul. So, I'm good. Besides, it's about time I got my own place for Xavier's sake. He needs to see his dad being a grownup and providing for him. We both know I've been slacking in that area for far too long now."

"You're a good father, Robbie."

"I know. I never said I wasn't. I'm just saying that I need to get out on my own. I need to step up my game."

"Fair enough. And you sure you're good with..." I

gesture toward him, hoping he'll fill in the blank. Talking money with your friends is always awkward.

"Do you have any idea how much I've saved living with your ass when you wouldn't let me pay for shit? Yeah, Zach. I'm good."

I steer the car into a lot and pull into a parking space, pushing the car into park.

"Good. Now, get the fuck out of my car. I have supplies to pick up."

"You're either insane for doing this, or you're a damn genius."

"I'm going with genius."

He pushes open the door and steps out.

"Make good choices! And for the love of all things holy, wear a fucking condom, man."

Robbie flips me off and slams my door closed, cutting off my laughter. He strolls into Lola's, his choice of establishment this fine Valentine's Day, and I silently remind myself to shoot him a text later to give me a call if he needs a ride.

I pull out of the lot and head to my next destination, wanting to rub my hands together with glee.

Delia's going to love this.

The doorbell chimes throughout the house and all I hear is the bleating of goats because they know Mama has arrived.

I race the Nigerian Dwarf goats, nearly tripping over them as I try to pull open the front door.

Delia jumps up and down and claps her hands at the sight of them, just as in love as she was the day we got them.

"Hi babies! Mama's here!"

She drops to her knees right there on the porch and lets the goats swarm her, giving them rubs and hugs and kisses.

"Ah, I see how it is. Buy a girl some goats and she'll leave you for them."

"Maybe you should try being as cute as them from time to time." She grins up at me.

"I *am* as cute as them. Hell, even cuter."

"Whatever helps you sleep at night."

She stands, herding the goats inside as I shut the door behind her. I pull her into my arms, gripping her by the waist and hugging her close to me.

She lets out a squeal of delight just as I press my lips to hers.

I take my time giving her the best first Valentine's Day kiss I can, moving my lips over hers in seduction. Her body begins to melt against mine and I tighten my grip on her before she goes down.

"Hi," she says breathlessly when I finally pull away.

"Hey gorgeous."

"Gorgeous, huh? What do you want?"

I let her go, laughing. "Nothing. Just complimenting my girl."

"*Gorgeous. My girl.* Yeah, you want something. I'm not doing anal, Zach."

I point a finger at her. "That is not what you said last week!"

"I said *maybe*."

"It's a special occasion, Delia. There's never a better time for maybes than special occasions."

"No. Butt. Stuff. Tonight."

"But butt stuff isn't completely off the table?"

She gives me a saucy grin. "We'll see."

"Glad you could see it my way." I wink. "Now, come on. Let's get this evening started. Let me put the kids away."

She bends down and gives them all pets. "Bye, my sweeties. I'll see you all later."

"I'm taking them outside. Why don't you pour us some wine? Or beer. Whatever you want, babe."

"Babe too?" she teases.

I laugh and corral the goats, pushing them out the back door and into their little house.

I make sure the latch the door tightly and then make my way back inside, praying Delia's still in the kitchen so she doesn't ruin the surprise.

My heart rate calms when I find her still pouring a glass of wine.

She slides a beer my way as she puts the bottle back into the fridge.

"How'd you know?"

"What? You thought I missed your not-so-subtle hint earlier?"

I grin at her and reach for her hand. "Come on upstairs. I have something for you."

"For me? A gift? Are we Valentine's Day gift people?"

"It's sort of a gift for me too."

"I already told you: no butt stuff."

"And I said we'll see."

"Zach."

"Delia."

"It's not butt stuff. It's something you'll love...I hope."

"Fine. You've convinced me. Lead the way."

I pull her behind me, leading her up the stairs. We pause at the top to move the baby gate I have up.

"What's that for?"

"It was necessary to keep the kids downstairs."

She eyes me warily.

"What?" I say. "You'll see. After you."

"After me?"

"Yep. Scoot. Don't want it to get cold."

Her brows scrunch together but she moves down the hall toward my bedroom. The lights are turned down low but the closer we the brighter the glow grows.

Halfway there she turns back and smiles at me. "Did you do rose petals?"

"Even better."

"Yeah?"

"Oh yeah."

She grins and keeps walking as I casually trail behind her.

When she rounds the entrance to my room, she lets out a loud laugh and I pick up my pace so I can see her delight.

She's bent over, shoveling the first piece of pizza into her mouth.

"You made me a trail of pizza slices?"

I lift my shoulder. "What can I say? I know the way to your heart."

She laughs and grabs the next plate and then the next until she's standing by the bed with six plates of pizza and nowhere to go.

"A heart-shaped pizza? Ohmygosh You totally love me."

Oh hell yes I do.

She peers down at the pizza on the bed again, her lips pulled back into a huge smile. I watch patiently as her eyes fall to the center of the pizza where the support sits.

Her gaze snaps to mine. "Is that…"

"Yeah."

"Are you asking me…"

"Yeah."

"Isn't it too soon?"

"Do you think it is?" I counter.

She chews on her lip, staring down at the key again. "I…" A pause. "No, I don't think so. It feels…right."

"Yeah?"

She nods. "Yeah. It feels *really* right."

I grin and stalk toward her, but she shakes her head when I'm almost there and I stop in my tracks.

"Say it."

"Huh?"

"I want to hear you say it," she tells me.

"You want a big fancy speech, huh?"

"Nah. Just ask."

"Delia, my food whore who I love with my whole damn heart, will you move in with me?"

She lifts a shoulder. "I'll think about it."

I race toward her, swooping her into my arms, a piece of pizza she was holding smashing against us while the rest falls to the floor.

Poor pizza.

She grins down at me. "I didn't know you were into food play. We could have brought this into the bedroom long before.

"Delia Devlin, mother of my goats, will you *please* move in with me? Pretty please?"

"You promise to let me eat pizza in bed at least once a week?"

"I..." *Fuck. I really don't want crumbs in there but for her...* "Yes.

"And I *always* get the last piece?"

"Yes."

"And you'll share your ranch?"

"You're walking a thin line, woman."

She leans down and presses a quick kiss to my lips. "I love it when you call me woman like that. You growl it and it's *so* sexy."

"Oh yeah?"

She nods.

"I'll call you woman every damn day if you move in with me."

She leans close again and whispers, "I was going to

say yes anyway, but deal."

I go to crush my lips to hers and she pulls back, pushing at me to let her down so I do.

"No way, mister. I like a clean house." She climbs into the bed and snags another piece of pizza, taking a bite. "Get to cleanin'."

"Get to cleaning? Seriously? It's Valentine's Day. I thought we could, you know, bang."

"Bang? Is *that* what we do?"

"Oh, we totally bang."

"Good lord, Zachary." She knows I hate it when she calls me that. "We're not banging until *all* this pizza is cleaned up."

"All of it?"

"Yep." She winks. "Oh, and strip."

Best. Valentine's Day. Ever.

THE END

Want to see what the Texting gang is up to lately?
Check out the **CAROLINA COMETS** series to catch up
with them!

Here's a preview of book one, **PUCK SHY**, a laugh-out-
loud spicy hockey romance where the hero and heroine
meet online (AKA more fun texting banter)…

PUCK SHY
CHAPTER 1

COLLIN

"No, no, no..."

Smoke billows from under the hood of my old beat-up Land Cruiser that has certainly seen better days. With a groan, I navigate it onto the shoulder, and just as I get the last tire off the main road, the car dies completely.

Dread sinks into my gut.

I'm more capable of handling a hockey stick than a wrench, but even I know smoke like this isn't a good sign.

I sigh and yank up the emergency brake, then slam my hand against the steering wheel in frustration. I've already been stranded in a podunk town for two days while I had to wait on new tires to be delivered to replace my two popped ones.

Now, less than four hours from home, I'm fucked again.

I knew driving the old beater vehicle across the country probably wasn't the best idea. I should have listened to my pops when he suggested I flatbed it. He knew the car wouldn't make the trek from the middle of nowhere Kansas all the way to North Carolina.

I was determined to have the last few days of my break to myself though. Just me and the open road, nothing but my thoughts to keep me company.

Turns out that was a bad idea too because my thoughts suck as much as this car does.

The end of last season has been on perpetual repeat in my brain, and I've spent the entire drive thinking of all the things I could have done differently to not cost us the Stanley Cup.

Such as not taking a penalty just moments before the end of the tied regulation, which led to a goal *and* the loss of Game Six in overtime. After we won Game One, we were feeling good, ready to take it to the end. But after losing Games Two, Three, and Four—in overtime, no less—we were feeling defeated. We rallied for Game Five and barely scraped by with a win, but that spark was back. Then Game Six happened and we folded like a house of cards at the last minute, blowing the series.

It was a total punch to the heart.

I wish I could say that was the worst of it for me.

A car speeds by, shaking the SUV and pulling me from recalling one of the worst moments of my life.

I don't need to take a trip down memory lane. Right now, I need to figure out what the hell I'm going to do to get back home. Coach expects the team to report tomorrow at 8 AM, and after letting him down last season, I can't be late. This year *has* to go better than last. I have a contract on the line. I need to get my shit together, prove I'm worth the time and money. I want to stay with the Comets, and I'll do whatever it takes to make that happen.

I pop the hood and hop out of the car to take a look at the damage.

When I peer in at the engine, it's obvious I'm not going anywhere anytime soon. There's errant fluid, and a low hiss echoes on the otherwise quiet road; it's coming from around where the smoke is rising.

A tow is definitely in order.

I wipe my hands off on my jeans—something my mom would kill me for if she saw me—and round the car to grab my phone from the cup holder.

I search for the nearest mechanic and hit GO on the results.

And I wait.

Then wait some more.

Nothing.

There's not enough service to get the results to load.

I walk up and down the road, but it's no use. I'm in the middle of nowhere. There's nothing for miles.

With my frustration growing, I trek back to my car and survey the area. I'm not sure what I'm looking for. A rescue maybe? I didn't pass many cars when driving, so I'm not expecting anyone to come flying down the road anytime soon.

I'm about an hour and a half from sunset, maybe less, and I think there was an exit about five or so miles back. If I hustle, I can probably make it before it gets too dark out.

"Fuck it," I mutter to nobody but myself. "I'll walk."

Hell, maybe it'll be good for me. Help clear my head.

I grab my wallet from the center console and a flashlight out of the glovebox just in case I need it, then lock up the car.

I shoot off a text to Rhodes, the one guy on the team who doesn't want to choke the shit out of me, hoping it'll go through eventually and he can send someone to help.

I slip my phone into my back pocket and, somehow —despite having done it a hundred times before—I miss.

The overpriced hunk of metal crashes to the ground. I don't even have to pick it up to know the screen is shattered because that's just the kind of luck I have lately.

Not that I give a shit about the phone being broken. I can buy another with no problem.

My issue is that everything that could possibly go wrong since blowing the Cup has gone wrong.

The week after we lost, a few guys from the team—the ones still talking to me—got together at a local bar to drown our sorrows. After one too many drinks were slung around, a brawl ensued after I witnessed some asshole manhandling a woman.

I did the right thing. I stepped in and handled shit.

But guess who got slapped with the cuffs after it was all said and done?

Me. That's fucking who.

Luckily the asshole ended up dropping the charges when the truth about what started the fight came out.

The damage was done though. I was branded a hothead when the press began digging into my past, and a file that should have been clean suddenly wasn't.

Two arrests for assault? Not a good look on the team.

With my name and face being splashed across headlines and social media, Coach suggested I lie low for the summer, get my head on straight before the upcoming season. So, I packed my bag and headed out west to my parents' farm.

The flight out to my parents' house? Rescheduled… twice. To top it off, my luggage was lost, and I ended up having to wear my brother's too-small clothes the first three days I was there.

Mom forgot to mention she turned my old bedroom into an office, so I crashed on the same lumpy, uncomfortable couch we've had since I was in middle school. At six foot three, the couch is the last place I need to be sleeping. That first week home was spent with a kink in my neck, and I swear it's still fucked up.

That was just the beginning of the shitstorm that would follow.

I thought going back home for the summer would be good for me, thought being away from the city I let down would be for the best. I could put the loss and the gossip behind me and get my mind right. But everything that could go wrong did, and the more shit went wrong, the more I couldn't help but think it was all my fault somehow.

I pinch my nose between my fingers, inhaling and exhaling slowly to remain calm.

Figuring shit out under pressure isn't typically a

problem for me. You don't become a first-round draft pick in the NHL by not being able to handle the heat.

But today, my ability to stay cool is being tested beyond belief.

First my car, now my phone.

"Can't just *one* thing go right for a change?"

With a huff, I snatch my phone off the ground to assess the damage.

As expected, the screen is toast. But the real kick in the nuts?

It won't turn on.

"Just fucking great." Now if my text did somehow go through to Rhodes, he's not going to have any way to get ahold of me.

Fury races through me and I want nothing more than to smash the useless device against a tree, but I refrain.

Instead, I set off down the road again, keeping my head down, making sure to stay far away from the two-lane highway. The sky grows darker a lot faster than I anticipated, and I've misjudged either how long I have until sundown or how far back this exit is.

I walk about a mile before I see headlights pop over a hill in the distance. Whoever it is, they're flying.

And that worries me because the closer they creep to the edge of the road, the closer they're getting to me.

Does the universe hate me so much that I'm about to get mowed down in the middle of nowhere with nobody to witness it? Where they likely wouldn't find my body for days?

The driver isn't showing any sign of slowing or moving over.

I slow my gait as they approach, ready to jump out of the way if I have to. And I really fucking think I'm going to have to.

Just when I'm sure I'm going to have to dive into the ditch for safety, a loud squeal pierces the air as they slam on their brakes, fishtailing all over the road.

The car skids another thirty yards or so before coming to a complete stop.

I'm paralyzed.

I can't move. Can't look away from the car that's now just sitting in the middle of the road.

What the hell just happened?

The sky is still bright enough that I can see the driver's form in the car. Can see them sitting there unmoving, likely in the same state of shock I'm in.

Finally, they shake their head and ease their foot off the brake.

Are they just going to drive away? After they almost hit me? Just like fucking that?

I take two steps toward the vehicle, ready to—*fuck*, I

don't even know what I'm going to do. Yell at them? Chase them down? That'd be stupid. Plus, I don't need to get in any more trouble than I'm already in.

But I'm *pissed*. Who almost hits a person, then just drives off like it's nothing?

I stop walking when the car slowly eases onto the shoulder and the driver kills the engine.

Guess they are going to stop after all.

I wait for whoever it is to make the first move. To roll down the window and ask if I'm okay. To get out and apologize. To do anything other than sit there. It's too dark to see into the car completely, but I can feel them staring at me in the rearview mirror.

I stare back, my anger growing by the second.

I swear it's hours before the door finally pops open.

"What the hell is your problem?" I lay into them the moment the door is ajar. "Do you have any idea how close you were to hitting me? You could have kil—"

I try to rein in my surprise when a woman who can't be more than five foot five steps out of the car and turns to face me.

She shoves long, wavy strands of hair out of her face. She's still a good twenty feet away, but I can see the shock in her eyes from here. Her jaw is dropped, hands shaking at her sides.

She takes a step toward me. Then another.

She stops at the back of her car and stares at me with wide eyes.

But it's not the same wide-eyed stare I get from fans. There's no sign of recognition on her face.

She looks terrified out of her mind. Like she's scared of me.

Ridiculous considering I'm the one who almost got dead.

We stare at one another for several beats, not saying a peep. It's calm out here, not much of a breeze. Nothing to fill the silence between us except her quiet breaths.

I don't know what the etiquette is here. Just moments ago I was ready to lay into her, but the look she's giving me...

"I, uh..."

A pause.

Ten seconds pass.

"I..." She tries again, her tongue darting out to wet her lips. She pulls the bottom one between her teeth, trapping it there while she mulls over what she's going to say next.

A sigh.

And finally, "Are you okay?"

Her voice is soft. Timid.

I nod.

"I...I didn't see you. And then I did. But I thought...I thought you weren't real."

I tilt my head. "Not real?"

My voice comes out gruffer than I intend, probably from not talking to anyone for so long. She looks as surprised as I do by the sound of it.

"You know, the stories about this road. I thought you were the Ghostly Drifter."

"Ghostly Drifter?"

I have no fucking clue why I'm just repeating the ends of her sentences.

She doesn't seem to mind.

"You haven't heard the stories?"

I shake my head.

She wrings her hands, eyes darting around, taking in the heavily wooded area around us. "Well, supposedly, along this stretch of highway, a drifter roams. He's said to show up around dusk, and he only appears to people who are alone. He flags you down, claiming his car broke down, and asks for a ride. If you let him into your car, you're giving him permission."

"Permission for what?"

"To eat your soul. It's said he absorbs all the good parts of you, leaving all the bad behind. Everyone who has reported picking him up has committed a horrific crime in the weeks following."

"That...sounds like a load of shit."

She huffs out a laugh. "But I've never seen anyone wandering these roads before tonight, and well..." She lifts her shoulders. "Freaked me out. Probably because I was listening to *Strange, Dark, and Mysterious.*"

"You listen to Johnny?"

Her eyes widen with shock and she grins. "You're a fan of the podcast?"

"I listen to him all the time during..." I pause, not wanting to reveal too much about who I am. I have no idea who this woman is. She's not showing any signs of recognizing me, but she could be playing me. It wouldn't be the first time it's happened. "When I'm on a plane," I finish.

"Fly a lot?"

"Sometimes more than I'd like."

Silence falls between us again, and she's back to wringing her hands. She's nervous, but I can't tell if it's me making her feel that way or that we both just almost experienced a life-altering thing.

"I...I really am sorry," she says quietly. Her voice is barely above a whisper, but it carries over to me with ease.

I'm just now realizing how quiet this stretch of the road really is. And after her story—even though it's total bullshit—it's kind of creepy being out here.

"What are you doing out here?"

"My car broke down."

A soft squeak leaves her lips, and I can't help but chuckle.

"I'm not the drifter guy, I promise."

Her eyes narrow. "That sounds exactly like what he'd say."

"Well, I guess the only way you'll know is to let me into your car."

Her face falls, and she takes a step back from me.

"Fuck." I lift the backward cap on my head, running a hand through my hair before replacing it. "That sounded creepy as shit, didn't it?"

She nods.

"Look," I say, taking a step toward her. She steps back again, and I pause, realizing I'm likely scaring the crap out of her right now. "I've been on the road since six this morning, and now my car is broken down. I tried calling for a tow truck but lost signal. Then I dropped my phone, and because nothing these days is made like it once was, it's broken. So now I'm stranded. I saw an exit a couple of miles back and was walking that way when I almost got run over."

She grimaces, her face telling me she's sorry for that.

"It's just been a long day," I tell her. "I'm tired and frustrated and just want to get where I'm going so I can crash. So thanks for not hitting me. I'm fine. You're fine." I toss my thumb over my shoulder. "I'm going to get going before I lose any more light."

I turn on my heel and shove my hands into my pockets, keeping my head up just in case someone else decides to come barreling down the hill and almost kill me.

What a fucking day.

And now I'm going to be out here in the pitch dark.

Fuck do I hope my flashlight doesn't give out on me.

"Wait!"

I hear the crunch of gravel under her shoes as she gets closer.

I spin back around, waiting.

"I..." She sighs. "That exit you saw? That's at least fifteen miles back."

"What? Are you sure?" I could have sworn it wasn't more than two miles.

But everything out here does look the same...

She nods. "I've driven this road a hundred times. It's the exit for Springsville. The next exit that way"—she points the way she was heading—"is another ten miles." She drops her hand, tucking it into her back pocket and rocking back on her heels. "We're in a really rural area, and the cell service is notorious for being nonexistent. You picked a really bad place to break down."

Awesome. Good to know I was walking in the wrong direction.

"Where are you headed?"

It's on the tip of my tongue to tell her, but I don't think that would be the smartest thing to do. For all I know, *she* could be the Ghostly Drifter.

Don't be an idiot, Col. There's no such thing as ghosts.

"Near Jonesville," I say instead. It's not exactly where I'm going, but it's a town over.

"I'm headed to Bartlett. That's on my way..."

Is she... "Are you offering to give me a ride all the way there?"

She shrugs. "I *did* almost run you over. It only seems right."

"I could be dangerous."

She tips her head to the side, watching me closely.

I can't clearly see the color of her eyes from here, but I'm betting it's something brilliant.

"I don't think you are."

I'm not, but... "You don't know me."

"Are you trying to convince me that you *are* dangerous?"

"No. I just think that since—"

"I'm a woman, I'm helpless and incapable of handling myself?" She crosses her arms over her chest, cocking her hip out. She stares at me with hard eyes. "I have a gun in my glovebox."

She looks so tough right now, like she isn't going to take this from me. I like that she's standing up for herself, but still... "I wasn't going to say that. But also, you shouldn't tell me where you keep your weapon."

She tucks her lips together. "That's fair. Though I could be lying about it..."

I get the feeling she's not.

"Do you want a ride or not?"

I really hate that she's offering a ride to a complete stranger, but I'm glad the complete stranger is me.

"It's a Sunday," she says. "Repair shops are going to be closed. What are you going to do? Try to hang around some place until someone can come get you?"

Hanging around in public for hours doesn't sound appealing. I have no fucking clue where I am and now no phone to get ahold of someone.

"All right," I agree. "A ride would be great. I can call for a tow later."

She gives me a single nod and heads for the car.

We make it four steps before she whirls around again.

This time I'm much closer to her, the closest I've been yet.

Her eyes are bright blue, so bright they're almost

white. Her lips are pouty and full, the bottom one just slightly larger than the top. Her nose is small and upturned at the end, but not in a distracting way. It's...cute.

She's *cute*.

"What's your name?"

"Huh?" I draw my eyes away from her mouth, back to her eyes that are trained on me with caution.

"Your name?"

"It's...Collin."

"Why didn't you sound sure of that? Is that a fake name?"

"It's not." I'm just not entirely used to someone not knowing who I am. "My name is Collin. My friends call me Col." I leave out my last name on purpose.

"Collin." She tests my name on her lips, like she's trying to decide if she likes it or not. She sticks her hand out to me. "Harper."

"Nice to meet you, Harper." I take her hand in mine, noting how small it is compared to my giant paws. Her skin is soft too. "Thank you for not running me over."

A grin pulls at the corner of her lips. "Come on. We still have about a four-hour drive ahead of us."

"Uh, should I drive? I'm not entirely sure I trust your night vision."

Those white-blue eyes narrow. "Gun, remember?"

"Right, in the glovebox. I remember."

She turns on her heel, making her way to the driver's side of the little white Honda.

That's when I spot it.

A Carolina Comets bumper sticker.

Fuck me.

She really didn't seem like she recognized me at all, but maybe she's just a really good actress? I have nothing to base that on. I don't know her. Which makes me even more of an idiot for willingly getting into the car with her.

She must notice me hesitating.

"Are you memorizing my license plate?"

I already did. "No. I, uh, noticed the sticker. Hockey fan?"

She lets out a single laugh. "No. Not into sports at all. It came with the car." She lifts her shoulders. "Are you?"

"You could say I'm a fan."

"Oh great." She rolls her eyes as I make my way to the passenger door. "Just please don't talk my ear off about it the entire drive or I'm likely to fall asleep at the wheel."

This is going to be a long four hours.

PUCK SHY
CHAPTER 2

HARPER

You never realize how long a mile is until you're sitting in silence with a stranger you just almost hit with your car.

I am now well aware of just how much it feels like forever as the quiet stretches between us.

Holy shit. I can't believe I almost hit someone.

I *really* can't believe that same someone is now sitting in my passenger seat.

And I lied to him.

There's no such thing as the Ghostly Drifter.

I was totally screwing around with my stereo, trying to get my auxiliary cord to sit right so my podcast would stop cutting out. But making up some story felt better than admitting I was one of those assholes who play with their phone while they're driving.

I steal a glance over at him.

He's tall, so tall that when he folded himself into the car, his knees were against the dash. He leaned the seat back so his head wasn't brushing the ceiling too. His shoulders are wide, and he's taking up every inch of his side of the car and some of mine.

He's turned his baseball cap forward, and I'm a little disappointed by the way it covers his eyes. They're a bright green, and I'm sad I won't ever get to see them in the daylight because I'm betting the color is gorgeous.

His hands are big too as they rest on his jean-clad thighs. They're veiny, but not in that way that's *too* veiny. More in the way that a nurse would look at hands and think, *Wow. That's some serious nurse porn right there.*

I'm trapped in this car with this gorgeous man who smells like leather and something else I can't quite place my finger on.

He's sitting so still it's making me uncomfortable.

"So, how far up here is your car?" I shift around, trying to make conversation.

"I think a mile or so. Do you mind if we stop at it real quick? I need to grab my bags." He huffs out a laugh that contains zero humor. "I really thought I was going to be able to walk to a service station or something and get this taken care of tonight, but that's clearly not going to happen."

It really wasn't.

I didn't lie when I told him we're practically in a dead zone for cell service.

I've driven through these parts enough times in the last three years to know that. I just came from spending the weekend at my mom's to celebrate my sister's engagement to her lawyer fiancé.

Something my mom made sure to bring up every second of the trip.

"I just don't understand why you don't settle down, Harper."

"You should find a successful man like your sister, Harper."

"You're scaring off suitors with all those creepy things you make, Harper."

She means well. I know she does.

But when you watch your parents love each other for sixteen years and then discover that the reason your father died suddenly in a car crash was because he was on his way to visit his mistress...

Well, it kind of screws with you and puts you off relationships.

"Are you from around here?" Collin's deep rumble pulls me from my thoughts.

"Sort of. I'm from Howardsville, but I've lived in Bartlett since I graduated college."

"What's with all the *villes* in this area? I swear every city ends in *ville*."

I laugh. "I thought I was the only person who ever noticed that. It drives me nuts. It's confusing." I glance at him. "Are you from here?"

He takes his time answering but finally says, "No. I'm from Kansas."

"Really? What are you doing all the way out here?"

"Work." He doesn't elaborate, just points up the road. "My car is just over this hill."

A wave of relief flows through me when we reach the top and it's sitting on the side of the road.

At least he wasn't lying about being stranded. That makes me feel marginally better about letting a strange man into my car.

I wasn't lying when I said he doesn't seem like the dangerous type. Maybe that's just me being hopeful and naive, but I'm generally good at reading people.

I pull to a stop behind his SUV. It's not as nice as I expected it to be. He's only wearing a pair of jeans and a t-shirt, but even I have enough fashion sense to see that neither item cost less than a hundred dollars.

Which is insane. I think my entire outfit cost me ten. I love a good clearance rack.

"I'll be right back," he says quietly, but he doesn't make any move to exit the car.

I glance over to find him staring at me expectantly, like he's waiting for confirmation that I'm not going to leave him on the side of the road or something.

"I'll be here," I say reassuringly, trying to pretend I don't love the way the dome light casts shadows across his face. I kill the engine to prove to him I'm not going to leave.

He gives me a single nod, then pushes the door open. He jogs to the vehicle and opens the back door. There's not much, a few bags.

One of them is massive and looks like it weighs nearly half of me, but he slings it over his shoulder with zero apparent effort.

He grabs the other two, then pushes the back door closed with his elbow.

I pop my trunk and climb out of the car to meet him.

He's staring down at the Carolina Comets sticker on the bumper, and I wonder if I offended him by not being a fan of hockey. It's not like I'm anti-sports or anything, they just don't exactly get my nipples hard.

I pause just as I'm about to lift the trunk, remembering what I have in there. I pin him with a glare that I hope is fierce. "Do not judge me for the contents of my trunk."

"As long as it's not a body, I think we're good."

When I wince—because it's not a body per se—he arches a dark brow but doesn't say anything.

Huh. Awfully trusting.

I lift the trunk and hold my breath, waiting for his reaction.

He laughs, and it's a deep, throaty sound that I'm going to pretend I don't find attractive.

"Hey! I said not to judge me."

"I didn't promise not to." He slides his eyes toward my trunk. "You going to move these creepy-as-fuck things or what?"

"They are not creepy!" I reach into the trunk to grab a box of dolls to move to the backseat. "Well, fine. They are kind of creepy. But that's the point of them."

"Please tell me you don't collect these."

"For personal use? No. But I do use them to make decor."

"You...make stuff with these?"

I nod as I pull open the back passenger door. "I have a store online that specializes in these. I make and sell other stuff too, but these always make a big profit, usually because I can pick them up so cheap."

I shove the box across the backseat to my side.

"What do you make out of them?" he asks when I reemerge to grab the other box.

"All kinds of stuff. Pretty much anything creepy. I'll usually paint them to look dead or like zombies. Sometimes I'll use them as a base to make baby versions of popular horror icons, like Michael or Jason or Freddy."

"That is..." I wait for him to make the same face a lot of people do. "Well, it's pretty fucking awesome."

"Yeah?"

"Hell yeah. I love old-school horror films like that. They don't make them like they used to, that's for sure."

"Right? They aren't even scary anymore, just rely on jump scares you can see coming from a mile away."

I grunt when I grab the second box so he can drop his stuff into the trunk. It's much heavier than the first, and I can already feel sweat beginning to form on the back of my neck. I'm sure I look real attractive right now.

"Totally not scary." He sets his three bags in the trunk, then grabs the box of doll parts from my hands. I want to protest, but something tells me he wouldn't let me carry it anyway. "Did you see the one with the ghost hunters?"

"The ones who turned out to be dead the whole time?"

"Yeah."

He rolls his eyes, then disappears into the backseat momentarily. When he reappears, he places his arms on the hood of the car and runs his hand over the stubble that's lining his sharp jaw. Shit, when did that move become hot?

"What about the one with the family who moved into the farmhouse and they ended up being stalked by the farmhand who showed up literally every time something creepy happened and they never put two and two together?"

"That one had me raging at the screen. Like, come on! First, why do you move into a house where a double murder happened and then act all surprised when spooky stuff starts taking place? Second, he was literally there every time! It was obviously him!"

He chuckles. "So awful."

We grow quiet, the faint sounds of insects beginning to come to life in the nearby forest.

Even though we're not speaking, I don't feel like I need to fill the silence. It's weird how easy it is to talk to him, but I'm also thankful because we have a solid four hours ahead of us.

"So, uh, is that everything you need from your car?"

He nods instead of answering, then reaches his hand across the hood.

"What?"

"Keys."

"What? No way."

"Yes way," he says as he pushes off the car and comes around to my side. He doesn't stop until he's right in front of me, and I have to tip my head back to look at his face. "I saw the way you were squinting just driving to my car. You're blind as fuck. You almost hit me when there was still light outside. We're about half an hour from there being none at all, and I'd really like to get to where I'm going in one piece."

I grit my teeth because he's not wrong.

I am blind as fuck at night. It's why I was so annoyed when my mom insisted we go for lunch with my sister this afternoon. It ran long just like I knew it would and put me a good two hours behind when I wanted to leave to avoid driving at night.

"You can trust me, Harper."

I stare up at him, and my mouth goes dry.

Can I trust him?

I don't know why I'm hesitating all of a sudden, why just now my nerves are on edge.

Maybe it's the reality that I'm about to drive multiple hours with someone I don't know sitting beside me. Someone insanely attractive on top of it.

Or maybe it's that handing him my keys is like handing over my life to him.

I drop them into his outstretched hand. "If you wreck my car, I swear, I'll—"

"Shoot me with your gun?"

"Yes!"

That part I didn't lie about. I do have a gun.

"Right," he says, not looking the least bit threatened. "Duly noted. Let's get on the road, then."

I march over to the passenger side and climb into my car. It feels weird being on this side of the vehicle, and not just because I have to pull the seat way up.

The car isn't much to most people, but it's mine and it's completely paid for, which is a big bonus in my eyes. I wanted something reliable, and this has proved to be just that.

Granted, I didn't think it was that small when I bought it, but I know it just feels that way now because of Collin taking up most of the room.

I watch the way his muscles jump as he navigates us back onto the road. He looks calm and collected—and a lot more confident driving than I did as night falls around us.

Several miles pass before either of us speaks.

"Do you do it full-time?"

My brows pinch together at his question, and he peeks over at me when I don't answer right away.

"The dolls," he clarifies. "Is that what you do full-time?"

I nod. "It is. I went to school for art and found I had a knack for creating props and such."

"Wouldn't that be a job more suited for California? Hollywood and such?"

"Ever heard of the internet?" I cringe at the sarcasm that drips from my words. "Sorry. I'm not exactly good with people, and sometimes my words come out a little harsher than I intend."

"I mean, my first impression of you was you trying to run me over. Little hard to top that at this point."

Another cringe. "Sorry."

He laughs. "All good. You're more than making up for it by giving me a ride. My co—boss would probably have my ass for getting in a car with someone I don't know, but I bet he'd be even more pissed if I was roadkill."

"I doubt you would have died. I wasn't even going that fast."

He gives me a look that clearly says I'm full of shit before returning his gaze to the road.

"Fine." I huff. "So you'd maybe be a little dead. I'm really glad I didn't kill you though. That would have looked so bad for my business."

"Yes, your business being in jeopardy was my biggest concern too."

A smile tugs at his lips.

Maybe my surprise road trip buddy won't be so bad after all.

Want more?

PUCK SHY is now available in Kindle Unlimited, paperback (two versions—guy edition and special edition), and in audio!

OTHER TITLES BY TEAGAN HUNTER

CAROLINA COMETS SERIES

Puck Shy

Blind Pass

One-Timer

Sin Bin

Scoring Chance

Glove Save

Neutral Zone

ROOMMATE ROMPS SERIES

Loathe Thy Neighbor

Love Thy Neighbor

Crave Thy Neighbor

Tempt Thy Neighbor

SLICE SERIES

A Pizza My Heart

I Knead You Tonight

Doughn't Let Me Go

A Slice of Love

Cheesy on the Eyes

TEXTING SERIES

Let's Get Textual

I Wanna Text You Up

Can't Text This

Text Me Baby One More Time

INTERCONNECTED STANDALONES

We Are the Stars

If You Say So

HERE'S TO SERIES

Here's to Tomorrow

Here's to Yesterday

Here's to Forever: A Novella

Here's to Now

Want to be part of a fun reader group, gain access to exclusive content and giveaways, and get to know me more?

Join Teagan's Tidbits on Facebook!

Want to stay on top of my new releases?

Sign up for New Release Alerts!

TEAGAN HUNTER writes steamy romantic comedies with lots of sarcasm and a side of heart. She loves pizza, hockey, and romance novels, though not in that order. When not writing, you can find her watching entirely too many hours of *Supernatural*, *One Tree Hill*, or *New Girl*. She's mildly obsessed with Halloween and prefers cooler weather. She married her high school sweetheart, and they currently live in the PNW.

www.teaganhunterwrites.com

www.ingramcontent.com/pod-product-compliance
Lightning Source LLC
Chambersburg PA
CBHW061548310726
48972CB00008B/2660